Books and Suits

A friends-to-lovers romance

S.C. Principale

Dedication:

To my incredible husband, who makes writing happy endings a matter of personal experience.

To my writing family : Judy, Rachelle, Katherine, Kathleen, Hebi, Sofia, Lois, Terry, Michelle, Dawn, Jen, Susan, Annee, and so many more.

ALSO BY S.C. PRINCIPALE

Contemporary Romance/Romantic Suspense
Passion: Sisters of Sin Femme Fatale Series[1]
Repairs[2]
Turning the Tables[3]
It's Business, Baby: Mature, Curvy Erotic Romance[4]
The Lady of the House: Mature, Curvy Erotic Romance[5]
Chocolate Krinkles and Two Kris Kringles[6]
Belgravia Security: A Bodyguard Romance[7]

Paranormal Romance
Pale Girl[8]
CrossRealms: You an' Me Against the World[9]
CrossRealms: Healing Hope[10]

---

1. http://books2read.com/u/3n5DX6

2. http://books2read.com/u/br1oVZ

3. https://books2read.com/u/mv1R18

4. http://books2read.com/u/bPyG07

5. http://books2read.com/u/4jPooD

6. http://books2read.com/u/mVRwkJ

7. https://www.amazon.com/Belgravia-Security-A-Bodyguard-Romance/dp/B09DDHWF3C

8. http://books2read.com/u/bPQ0aJ

9. http://books2read.com/u/bwKrvP

<u>CrossRealms: Gestures</u>[11]
<u>CrossRealms: A Helpful Gentleman</u>[12]
<u>CrossRealms: Wicked Woods</u>[13]
<u>CrossRealms: Shattered</u>[14]
<u>CrossRealms: Mended</u>[15]
<u>CrossRealms: Whole</u>[16]
<u>Mountain Bound: A Monstrous Love Story</u>[17]
<u>Vampire in Vegas</u>[18]
The Man with The Umbrella (What Happens in Venice Anthology)
Historical Romance
<u>Alliance</u>[19]

10. http://books2read.com/u/4ApQoK

11. https://books2read.com/u/mlAJJA

12. https://books2read.com/u/3kPnER

13. http://books2read.com/u/m0B8GA

14. https://books2read.com/u/mBwEev

15. https://books2read.com/u/baDAPa

16. https://books2read.com/u/mKpo9d

17. http://books2read.com/u/bPQp6A

18. https://books2read.com/u/menE09

19. https://www.amazon.com/kindle-vella/story/B0B4F2RB94

Introduction

Amanda Gardella and Joel Martin were best friends growing up in the same suburban town. Secure in the knowledge that they could defy the stereotype that "boys and girls can't be best friends", they steadfastly resisted the lure of being high school steadies- even if they fed the rumor mill a little too much! They were sure they'd always have time for each other as adults- but Amanda followed the books- becoming a librarian at the local university. Joel followed the suits, leaving town to join a high-pressure investment firm in the city.

Time, distance, and a little bit of resentment that Books and Suits came between them, Amanda and Joel's close relationship dwindled to little more than wistful memories. Then, one day Joel's world gets turned upside down and he realizes there's only one person who can make things right again.

Chapter One

June, 2012

Amanda swayed, her brown-blonde wayward hair escaping from her up-do to join the smudgy mascara and make-up stains on Joel's white dress shirt.

"Are you seriously crying again?" he chuckled, patting her back with his smooth dark hand, soothing little circles as his scratchy goatee tickled her forehead.

"It's our last dance as high schoolers. In five days, we graduate. In five days, we're adults!"

"We've been eighteen for months, girl."

"Shut up, I'm nostalgic."

"Don't you have to be over eighty for nostalgia to set in?"

"Maybe you're thinking of dementia?" She sniffled and smiled at him, a crooked, teasing smirk. "I read that some people-"

"Here we go. Books again."

"Says the smart dude with the A in AP Calculus and a full-ride to Haven College of Business!"

"All 'bout the sharp suits and the big money, baby," he laughed and teased right back. That's how it was with Amanda. Ever since he moved in up the street from her in fourth grade, they'd been best friends. They joked together, laughed together, and got in trouble together.

"My God... I would glare at you but I can't see you properly." Amanda struggled to blink away her tears and all the annoying silver specks in danger of blinding her. She was tempted to retrieve her cat's eyes glasses out of her tiny, fashionable purse and rush to the restroom to scrub off the sparkly lash gunk her sister had talked her into trying.

Joel briefly looked concerned. His best friend was a total English nerd, a lit chick or whatever geeky title she'd proudly and loudly proclaimed for the week. He hadn't seen her without her glasses except when they went swimming at the beach every summer or when he showed up at her house way too early. "I wasn't going to ask but..."

"Laura wanted me to look 'glam' for the dance and prom pictures. Seeing as I almost never get dressed up..." She self-consciously tugged at the silvery-white gown which was held up by spaghetti straps and covered with light-catching sequins. She had a deep purple rose on her wrist and amethyst drop earrings adorning her ears. They matched Joel's killer purple tie and the single onyx and amethyst stud he had in his right lobe.

"I'll be glad when you move into dorms. She's a bad influence on you." He wasn't fully teasing. Laura was hot enough to turn every head on the street, but she was high maintenance, demanding, and liked to make people feel a little off-balance. How anyone as sweet as Amanda could have been raised by the same people who created Laura Gardella was beyond him. Although, he and his brother were certainly nothing alike. A.J. was sure the path to riches was achieved through hard work on the hardwood, while Joel knew it came from crunching the numbers and hustling.

Amanda sniffed in again, her eyes clearing this time. Joel was determined to become some big name, some tycoon in a Fortune 500 company. A shark, making dealings, making killings. With his dark eyes and his sharp features, she could see something predatory there. "What kind of influence am I?" Amanda asked.

When had the lights dimmed? Joel studied her face, wide hazel-flecked eyes, a beautiful, playful smile, staring up at him. She was sparkling. She was beautiful. "You're the best influence, Amanda. You know I—"

"Kiss her! Kiss her! Kiss her!"

He was seriously going to kill the jerks on the football team.

"Let's get out of here, Suits." Amanda tugged his hand and they escaped, leaving the prom early to a chorus of giggles and whispers about what the two of them were going to go do.

"THOSE GUYS HAVE KNOWN us forever! Just because we didn't have another date to the prom, they made all kinds of assumptions," Amanda washed her makeup off in the kitchen sink while Joel raided the fridge.

"Score! Your mom is an angel. Lasagne, baby!"

"Save some for my dad or he'll banish you from the house."

"He will not. I'm the son he always wanted."

"Ha. You're just the one who saves him from ever having to clean out the fridge."

"I'm deeply wounded and I'm telling on you when he gets home. Go take off your dress." Joel put the pan of foil-covered lasagne in the oven, at ease in the Gardella home as he was in his own.

Amanda froze, wet, wadded paper towels dragging across her lids. "Huh?" So, they'd never really talked about it, but maybe, just maybe, she'd been starting to notice that her best friend was truly one of the most handsome men in the world. Still, even if their platonic friendship was flooding the rumor mill, it truly *was* strictly platonic.

Completely oblivious to his poor wording, Joel was also taking out what was left of her mother's chocolate cake and searching for clean forks and plates in the dishwasher. "Go take the dress off so you don't get red stuff on it. You know you're a messy eater, Books."

"I am not! I just like messy food!" she retorted, relief restored.

Sort of.

"Joel?"

"Hm?"

"Can you unzip me a little? I can't—it's too hard to—"

He watched her wriggling in the skin-tight dress, her arm bending up the back to try to catch the minuscule zipper that was hiding between a sequined seam. "Sure thing. How far?"

"Right about here." She gestured to her mid-back.

HIS HEART WAS THUDDING a little too hard for his liking. Amanda was so pretty. More than pretty. Beautiful. Beautiful and curvy. Amanda was gorgeous and he was a horny teenager, dammit. He knew he should not have curious thoughts about her body. Yet, sometimes (like this very second) he did.

Joel stood so close to her that he felt her shift when his warm breath hit her bare shoulders. His fingers carefully slid the zipper down. He was silent. Joel wasn't silent unless math was involved, his mouth was totally packed or the NBA playoffs were happening. Now, he was afraid to open his mouth and let his thoughts escape. The zipper slid until it reached her fingertips. His warm cocoa skin melted over hers for a minute, touching her spine. He realized the dress was falling free now, sliding down her body. Amanda grabbed it hastily and held it tight to her bust as she made her escape upstairs.

"Be right back!" she called.

"Okay! I'm gonna start with dessert first!" He was eyeing the chocolate cake.

That sounded dirty in my head. Man, what's happening to me?

He'd folded Amanda's laundry before, with her help, quizzing each other on SAT vocab while stacking clothes in her laundry room. He'd seen her underwear. He'd seen her bras.

Never saw her in them, though.

Joel shifted uncomfortably. *Snap out of it.*

AMANDA RETURNED IN her Haven U. sweatshirt and pajama leggings. "I feel so much better." She stretched and wiggled her rather swollen-looking toes. "My feet are killing me, though. Heels were made by Satan."

"Yeah, I'm always complaining about that," he chuckled, serving himself a gargantuan slice of lasagne and giving her about half as much. "More?"

"Duh, yes. Sprite or Coke?"

"Coke."

When she turned around, Joel was shirtless. Of course. He didn't want to stain the rental. He wandered into the laundry room and returned wearing an old t-shirt of her dad's.

They ate in silence. Part of it was because she couldn't remember the last time she'd noticed that Joel had abs. Like— underwear model abs. When had that happened? Also, when had her stomach started to feel tight thinking about him?

"Everyone thinks we're in the backseat of your car right now," she muttered, an internal observation that escaped into the open air.

One choking fit later, Joel wiped his watery eyes and glared at her. "You could have waited until I was done eating."

"Then I would be an old, old lady." She calmly passed him a napkin.

"You don't care what the gossips say, do you? Everyone who really knows us knows that we're not—not doin' that. Your dad and mom would straight up murder me if they thought I was—"

"I think they'd be thrilled I had a good guy like you for a boyfriend. But no, they'd bury you in the backyard if you ate their lasagne *and* deflowered their daughter." *Oh, shit. Shit, shit, shit!*

For the second time that night, Joel was silent. "I thought you and Thomas might have..."

"Nuh-uh. He thought I was Laura 2.0." She shrugged, old heartbreaks shoved away, warmed by Joel's smile.

"Man was a damn fool. Give me the Amanda package any day." Joel beamed at her and patted her hand.

She sipped her soda hurriedly, blushing with pleasure. "It's for the best. He's going to UCLA, the other side of the country. Lots of our friends are already breaking up, like their love can't go the distance! He's one of them. He dumped Janelle."

"Carlos gave Min a promise ring and she gave it back when she got accepted to FSU."

They both stared at each other, having one of the unique moments that only best friends can share. "We're *so* much smarter than them, Books," Joel said.

"Way less drama, Suits."

"Bros before hoes." He held out his fist.

She bumped it. "Chicks before dicks. We gotta make something that works for boy-girl besties, you know that, right?"

"Umm... You and me before he and she?" he suggested.

"It needs work."

"Well, we have four years to perfect it." He raised his can to her. "To Haven University's newest English Education major, Amanda Gaaardellllaaa!" His voice boomed and faded around the room as if announcing the MVP walking onto the court.

She toasted him in return. "To Haven University's Haven College of Business All-Star, Joooo-el Maar-tin! Give it up, folks!"

As they cleaned up the food and put on Comedy Central, Joel let out a deep sigh. "I'm glad you're around."

"Hey. We're graduating, but we're sticking together. Okay?"

"Swear it?"

She gave him a three-fingered salute before she crashed next to him on the couch. "On my books and your suits."

Chapter Two

November, 2015

"Joel! Joel, Joel, Joel!" Amanda came tearing through the campus coffee shop to where Joel was sat, and waved a letter in front of his face.

He shifted, and she noticed his taut expression and the phone pressed to his clean-shaven face. "Hang on, Mom. It's 'Manda. What, Ma? Mom says hi."

"Hi, Renee! I'll see you on Saturday for book club!" Amanda pressed her head on top of Joel's to speak to her second mother.

"All right, Sugar. Make sure that boy eats something green, will you?"

"I'll try!"

"I'm sorry to hear about A.J.'s leg, Ma. I'll call him tonight, okay?" Joel hung up and groaned. "That dumb idiot. He tore his ACL, not even during a team workout, working out alone, no spotter, off-campus. It's not a 'school-related' activity or injury. The team might drop him and his scholarship." Joel suddenly looked years older, his sharp eyes exhausted as they met hers.

"Oh, no!" Amanda forgot her good news in the face of his troubles. "Can't they fix it? Surgery?"

"They can, but this is his senior year! This is *the* year. All the coaches who are studying the drafts are looking at players now, when he's going to be on the bench at best, off the team at worst."

"But he's not just there for basketball, he was working on a journalism degree, too!"

Joel's eyes closed. "Working on." Air quotes framed the words. "I thought that we, as the younger siblings, got to be the screw ups?"

"We keep breaking those stereotypes." First, by continuing to disprove that old saw that men and women can't stay friends without romance entering into it. Now, by being the "babies" that were actually making college and career a success. Not that Laura and AJ were struggling. Not exactly.

Laura was doing great, teaching yoga six days a week and doing fitness-wear modeling on the side. She made enough money to keep her in designer spandex and had a string of handsome boyfriends from her exclusive health spa to keep her in everything else. She went through trainers, hot members, golf pros, tennis pros, and forty-something sugar daddies who wanted a sexy, flexible girl to spoil.

Amanda's father and mother weren't speaking to Laura very much right now. Despite her sister's insistence that she wasn't sleeping with *all* of the men she was going through, her current method of paying the rent on her luxury condo hadn't sat well with her parents.

"They raised us to be more than our looks." Amanda helped herself to Joel's coffee with a savage slurp.

"Mom raised us to be more than some Black guys who were good at sports. The idiot!"

"Come on, anyone can get hurt."

"Not everyone half-asses his classes because he's *sure* he's going to make the draft! He's in a mid-tier college, in the middle of the pack of players, and he's short — well, he's short for the NBA."

"Joel—"

"I need a muffin." Joel stomped off and came back with two ooey-gooey cinnamon buns. "Eat."

Amanda ate. The predatory look in Joel's eye had turned up considerably since she'd seen him the day before. They ate in the dining hall together and hung out in one of their dorm rooms almost every night. People assumed they were a couple, even after numerous denials.

Right now, she wouldn't want to be this dude's girlfriend. Her best friend was always on the verge of a smile, his eyes about to twinkle. The man across the table had the same face, but the lightness was dimming. There was something cold in the way he devoured the pastry, the fork jabbing in hard, the knife dissecting layers of sweet dough.

"He's *not* gonna be a burden on our mother; another wannabe, another drop out," Joel seethed. "She's worked too hard to raise two sons alone, two Black males in this upper-middle class town, to put us through college... You wouldn't get it." A napkin was crumpled angrily in his fist.

"I know. I know I wouldn't get it." Amanda held out her hand. For the first time ever, Joel didn't take it.

"What's your news?" he asked after the cinnamon buns were nothing but crumbs.

"Oh! I got accepted in the library sciences program!"

Joel grinned at her squeal of excitement. "So— you'd be a librarian?"

"I hope so."

The grin was fading slowly, confusion in its place. "But you were going to be an English teacher."

"I know, but I just... I *want* this. I feel like it'd be more of a challenge. To get a job as a librarian, you have to be really good and stand out a—"

"That's right! It's way harder to get a job. To be a success. I mean, no offense, but libraries are dying out. I can just Google it. I can read it on my Kindle. Why do I need to go search it up in a book?"

"I'll pour hot coffee in your lap in a second," Amanda warned, genuine anger under the semi-serious threat.

"I'm serious, girl! High schools and middle schools all over the country need English teachers. Like— what, four or five per school?"

"Probably," she replied, her lips thin.

"But each school only needs one librarian. If that! My old school, before I moved here, didn't even *have* a library."

"Part of the reason your mom moved you from the city to the 'burbs, right? Better schools, better education. She wanted you to shine." *But you're not letting* me *shine. All you can think about right now is the money. The job. How your mom is busting her butt with double shifts at the hospital, how you and AJ busted your butts at practice, at school....* She was trying to be understanding.

"You can't just sit in your lilywhite tower reading about princesses and goblins all day, Books! The real world means that you—"

"Hey! Librarians help people find jobs, access resources, find books on subjects that they need information on. They hook you up with test prep materials, they help you research which kind of diet can help save your life, which treatment plans might help you knock your addiction or save your marriage!"

Her voice was raised..

He was standing. "In other words, everything you can do on a phone? A laptop?"

"Literacy is the most important—"

Joel talked over her, his voice angry, so angry and yet Amanda knew she wasn't really the target of his ire. "When you don't get hired because there's no market for your skills, what do you do? Put on your leotard and flex that bubble butt for the hot divorced guy in your chick lit club?"

The tiny splash of coffee was cold as she tossed her cup half-heartedly at him. She bolted from the coffee shop, pausing to look behind her at where Joel slowly wiped off his suit. His interview for an internship that afternoon seemed to be more important to him than the argument.

"HEY."

"Hi." Her eyes were wary as she held open the door and stepped back to let him in.

Joel immediately went to the narrow double bed in the tiny single dorm room, taking a seat on its stiff mattress. He placed his head in his hands, eyes searching for hers. "I was an ass."

"Yep."

"I'm sorry."

"I know you said things you didn't mean because you were worried about A.J."

He hesitated. They had been friends because they could say anything, but it always had to be true. "I was a jerk in the way I said it, but I did mean it, Amanda. I want you to live up to those booksmarts, girl! You need to make the right choices. Being a librarian sounds like a long-shot and being an English teacher is way more along the lines of a sure thing. I'm proud of you, but—"

"You don't think I can do it?"

When had his super smart best friend become as naive as his brother? His brother, who was hobbling around on crutches, frantically figuring out ways to bring up his 2.4 GPA so he didn't lose his athletic scholarship? His big brother, who was worrying about being back on the courts before March Madness, his last "big chance" to get noticed by NBA scouts.

"Amanda, let's look at this like an exponential growth equation. If you—"

"No," She cut him off, ice in her eyes.

"No?"

"This isn't like the millions of high school athletes who want to play in the major leagues. Library science isn't a dying profession, it's just a transforming one. I can *do* this. I can work in other jobs that don't require leotards until I get hired, too."

He groaned. "Oh, God. I'm *really* sorry."

"I'm *not* Laura."

"I know!"

"I'm not A.J., either!"

"I know, I know!"

"You're supposed to believe in me!"

"I believe you will get that degree in a heartbeat, 'Manda, I just don't want your dreams to get broken if you don't get the job that goes with it!" He walked over to her, her angular face somehow soft. He wasn't as tall as A.J., hovering just at six foot and so Amanda's head came to his shoulder as he enveloped her into a hug and laid a kiss on her messy bangs. "Not about how smart you are. It's about what's out there." She didn't know the world the way he did. It would eat you up and not think twice. "It'll kill me if your dreams get broken, too," he whispered.

Her eyes overflowed. "This isn't like the NBA. You never hear about a librarian being too old to play and needing to retire when she's forty. No career-ending injuries when I try to slam dunk a thesaurus onto a high shelf. I'm not going to lose my B.S. of English Education, either, okay? Library Science is a graduate degree. I got my acceptance letter today —contingent to when I graduate in May. I'll go right into the graduate studies program here at Haven." She flashed him a winning smile, out of step with her wet eyes. "Look at me go, huh?"

"Look at you go," he murmured. When was the last time she'd been swaying in his arms, with wet lashes and a wide smile?

"Prom. Senior prom." Amanda whispered, reading his mind.

HOW HAD HER BEST FRIEND looked so cold and calculating hours ago, and how was he so... warm right now? Joel's eyes were melting into hers, lips soft and fingertips softer as they traced her cheek and wiped away one last tear. His chest was a heating pad, warmth seeping into her skin through two layers of fabric, his hoodie and her pajama top.

"That's right. Three years later, still rockin' the best friends thing. Why didn't you tell me you were going to apply?"

The warmth was gone, on her end, not his. She gently pushed back, peering hard into his questioning eyes. "Joel, I mentioned grad school every day this semester. Remember? I told you I was going crazy trying to get the early admissions application done at the same time I was trying to cram for mid-terms?"

He winced. "Oops. I've been so—"

"Busy, I know." She bit her lip. Since they were being honest... "I think you need to work on some career-life balance. I have book club, we go to the rec center and use the gym sometimes, but you've been eating and sleeping business courses, business seminars, business podcasts, business journals... You're always cramming and the exams can't even catch up!"

"It's all about that hustle. I can't just sound like I know what's going on, I have to know what's going on. Look the look, walk the walk, talk the talk."

Amanda nodded. She had to admit that Joel radiated quiet cunning and success. He carried a leather satchel instead of a book bag, gold-topped pens and polished leather shoes instead of pencils and sneakers. "Are you gonna walk that walk right away from me? From Haven?"

Joel looked startled— then guilty.

Amanda knew there was something he hadn't told her. After being friends for so long, she knew the signs. "What is it?"

There was a moment of hesitation before Joel answered, "Nothing. You'll never lose me. I might have a little commute to the city, but I'll be around, you know that."

Amanda grinned when his hand suddenly found hers with an insistent tug. "Let's go back to my room and kill some Orcs?"

"For the horde!" she grinned.

IT FELT LIKE OLD TIMES, playing with him, knee to knee, screaming at each other to pick up the weapon, cover the flank, and grab the treasure.

Underneath, it felt like the old times were dying. Something was splintering, two paths diverging; a world of Books breaking free from a world of Suits.

"Will we always do this?" she whispered, hitting pause.

She watched him freeze like the character on the screen. His voice was soft as he leaned to brush his shoulder to hers. "Always. You know it, Books."

Chapter Three

M*arch, 2019*

Joel walked out of his office head held high, eyes steely as he walked with purpose through the busy metropolitan jungle. "Coffee, two sugars. To go." The lean man in a trim, dark suit and impeccable silk tie tipped handsomely for his usual mid-day caffeine boost.

"Our homemade Italian pastries?"

As usual, he refused, turning quickly. Every day, he went to the same shop. It was convenient and close to the firm of Hodge, Williams, and Henderson, where he was an up and coming assistant investment analyst. He had applied for the internship at Hodge, Williams, and Henderson, one of the largest investment firms in the Mid-Atlantic and landed it in January of his senior year. He'd maneuvered the internship into a job. After all, his Investment Seminar professor had worked at HW&H for ten years and said they only took the best, the quickest, and the sharpest. That's what he wanted to be.

He hadn't told Amanda that he'd applied util the papers were signed. He had a feeling that she would have objected to him joining a firm with a reputation for being sharp and cold, but that was the world he wanted to be in, no, the world he *had* to be in. That world didn't have a place for soft dreamers like Amanda.

But that didn't stop him from wishing.

Every day, as he allowed himself five minutes out of his glassy concrete fortress, he traveled not only through this city, but through the past, through the future, playing a game of what-if.

Today. I could call her today. Mom said she's doing fine. Laura's engaged. I could call to say congratulations. No, I'd call to say "About damn time!" Then we'd laugh.

He didn't laugh anymore, except when he was supposed to, at the unspoken behest of Mr. Hodge, Mrs. Williams, or Mr. Henderson. Or, when Vanessa said something that was supposed to be funny.

Vanessa was Mr. Hodge's only daughter. She had green eyes, caramel-colored hair, and mocha-almond skin. She looked like a supermodel. She dressed like a supermodel.

She was gorgeous, smart, and she wanted him.

She wanted Joel Martin, boardroom trailblazer, up and comer, a flint-eyed, ruthless analyst with perfectly maintained urban stubble, close-cropped waves, and suits that took up far too much of his salary.

She wanted Joel Martin, who went to see his mother a few times a month, but who spent almost every night crunching numbers and making calls. She liked when he made time for her, but she rarely asked him to put her before the job.

His fingers flexed on his phone. Vanessa had texted him a cute picture of their Valentine's ski trip. He sent back a smile emoji.

Vanessa was perfect for him.

So why wasn't he happy?

He had the perfect job with an enviable entrylevel salary. He'd paid for A.J. to get his ass in gear and finish the additional two years it took for him to get his degree in journalism. He was hustling and crunching numbers from nine in the morning until nine at night. Vanessa, raised by Mr. Hodge and a string of nannies, never seemed to mind that he put the office first and her second.

That's not the way it is when you love someone.

Every day, when he took his last sip of coffee, he put his phone back in his pocket. Every day, he still hadn't managed to call Amanda.

"PROFESSOR KLINE IS on the phone for you. *Ag-a-in*," Rhonda purred the message to Amanda as she flitted back to the stacks.

"That man. Robert!" she picked up her extension at the Haven University Library with a blush.

"How come all the hot college girls have crushes on me, but the eligible woman my heart desires is playing hard to get?" Robert Kline, a thirty-something Indiana Jones clone from the archeology department, inquired.

Amanda giggled. "Who said I was playing hard to get? I'm actually busy and it's your department's fault. Creating a whole new Museum Studies Department at Haven means a ton of grant proposals to write and new article subscriptions to get, not to mention curating the art collection and the—"

"Wow. I'm terrible. Look at me, keeping you so busy."

"I love it and you know it!"

"But do you love me?" he hinted—as he had hinted off and on for the last two months, about five months into dating.

She flushed. They still hadn't slept together. She told him she wanted to wait for the person she loved. She didn't know now if his desire to hear her say she loved him was based on his urge to merge, or because he really felt that way and wanted her to return his love.

"I love everything about you."

"Then you should let me take you to dinner as penance for keeping you so busy—or because you love everything about me, including the places I pick for our dates."

The flush grew. Dates. She hadn't really meant to start dating anyone. It was more like an accident. She'd been subbing at the schools while finishing her Library Science degree. She'd unexpectedly gotten hired as an assistant librarian at the university library within weeks of completing the program. The newly created department and the new library collection set off a ripple effect. The head librarian retired and spaces opened up throughout the staff. She applied. She got in. She worked hard and long to prove that they didn't make a mistake picking someone with almost zero experience. Robert Kline apparently felt the same way, eyed to head the new department before he was even forty. It was natural that two workaholics would run into each other at the library or the Museum Studies Department that was attached to it. Hastily grabbed coffees turned into working lunches. Working lunches turned into dinner and the movies.

She didn't want to be like Laura and string someone along. She'd always been so honest with-

Joel.

She'd been comfortable with Joel, because he was a best friend and they'd never dated. When things felt wrong with Robert, she told herself she was just being weird and comparing things that weren't meant to be compared.

Amanda had gotten a lot less honest since Joel slowly slipped from her life, another soul swallowed up in a world of Suits.

"I can't tonight. I'm sorry, Rob."

Silence. "Someone else? We never said we were exclusive but I kinda assumed and well, you know what they say. Ass. You. Me."

"I'm not dating anyone else. But that's all I'm ready for right now. Dating. Casual dating, if that's okay?"

Robert's voice was hurt, then bitter. "It's the age difference, isn't it?"

"No! Rob, no! You're so much fun and you're awesome and smart. I love being with you." *You remind me too much of someone I miss.* "I just think that you want more than I have to give. I'd love to hang out still?" she asked hopefully, heart curled up small and tight.

"Not just now. Thanks for being straight with me. I wish it'd happened a little sooner."

She put the phone down, her heart stinging from the sadness in Robert's voice. *So much for hiding with my books in a safe tower. I want to talk to Joel. The old Joel who would make me laugh, no matter how rotten I was feeling.*

Her face lifted slightly. She wouldn't be seeing Joel anytime soon, but Saturday was book club with Renee and her mom, the two greatest ladies on earth. Best of all, it was Renee's turn to host. When she knocked on the door, sometimes she pretended the last three years never happened. She pretended Joel would be there to open up the door and drag her inside and upstairs where they would eat junk, play video games, and study. Sometimes, lately, her fond recollections took a turn that she never expected. Turns that certainly weren't based on reality.

Her twenty-five-year-old self would suddenly envision all of the times they'd been left alone in their houses. Their parents had initially been cautious about leaving two attractive teens alone together, but as the years passed and it became obvious that Amanda and Joel were friends, not lovers, they relaxed.

Her mind replayed the night of the prom.

His hands on her zipper. What if she'd slowly slipped out of it right there in the kitchen? What if she'd told him to leave his shirt off?

She couldn't help but imagine what a perfect, beautiful first time they would have had. Joel was so warm back then, so comforting, ready to make her laugh, ready to uplift her. As for what she could do for him? Well, it was no surprise that his nickname for her was "Books." She loved to read. She read anything and everything she could get her hands on, including some of Laura's hidden paperback romances that had plenty of xxx-rated, steamy scenes. Around Joel, she would have been totally at ease, ready to try anything she'd read about, her pale skin and his dark skin making a beautiful yin-yang of flesh, her lips caressing his, caressing lower...

"Oh my God, Amanda! Are you okay?" Rhonda yelped, witnessing her fellow librarian panting as she clutched the wall for support.

"I'm—I had to—I just had a rough phone call. You head on home. I'll finish up here."

"BA-AAABE?" VANESSA sat on his black leather sofa (a gift from her), her long, smooth legs tucked under her. "Are you going to be done soon?"

"One more email." Joel hit send and turned around to see his girlfriend sitting there, in his bathrobe. He blinked. He was sure she hadn't been wearing that when she arrived bearing Chinese at— *Shit, three hours ago.* "Oh, man. I'm so sorry."

She giggled and pointed to the last unopened container on his coffee table. "You're a very lucky man. If I hadn't been used to Daddy saying 'one more phone call' or 'one more email' for my entire childhood, you'd be in hot water, mister."

"Mm, hot water sounds good. Think I'm gonna take a shower and call it a night. I can't believe your father scheduled a phone call with London for seven in the morning."

Vanessa's face took on a look of suppressed excitement.

He'd seen that look more often after their ski trip together. It was the first time they'd taken things to a physical level. Joel hadn't been entirely comfortable with the idea of sleeping with his boss's daughter. He wasn't sure he'd have been comfortable even if she hadn't been work-adjacent. She was older and more mature than him. Vanessa radiated worldliness and sophistication naturally, something he was still faking his way through, meaning his guard could never come down around her. Even if he'd been totally into her, totally at ease, they were supposed to be discreet about things according to the senior partners. He was relieved about that. He got the feeling Vanessa wasn't.

She was twenty-nine and he'd heard her say more than once that she wanted "a ring on it" by thirty. "I'm sorry about tonight. Reschedule?" He kissed her lips swiftly and sat in the recliner across from her.

"Jo-el," she purred at him again, opening the robe to reveal a lacy bra cup. "I won't let you oversleep."

"You know I love spending time with you, Baby, I just don't think we should spend the night together in your place or mine. It's not a good idea. People might think that I'm using you and I would hate that."

"I don't mind if you use me," she laughed, reclining, one calf sinuously caressing the leather backrest of the sofa.

"I got too far on my own. I'll be done with my M.B.A. next year and I'm going to leave the word 'assistant' in the dust." His jaw was set. Worked too damn hard with his brain and his hands to let anyone say his success at the firm was because he was Vanessa Hodge's toy boy.

Am I? Is that why they hired me?

No, no. Didn't even start dating Vanessa until a few months ago, I was already an intern when I was in college, hired straight afterward. Worked my way up.

When she saw that he was settled into his chair with a hard, faraway look on his face, she rose and came behind him, her fingers undoing the knots in his neck as he moaned softly. "That's right. No more assistant. You'll be the newest manager in Daddy's first international office, the London branch of Hodge, Williams, and Henderson."

Joel stood up so fast that Vanessa fell over the back of the chair with a screech. As he helped her up, ignoring the lithe body she was showing off under his robe, he demanded, "What? *London*? Vanessa, I'm not even thirty, there's no way in hell your dad would put me in charge of an international branch! Nor should he! I'd be the first one to tell him not to, it might look like someone too young and inexperienced is in charge of the firm's assets. That's bad for business." Joel paced away from her.

Vanessa followed, a petulant look on her face. "You won't be the only one there! You'll be his personal representative though, a sharp, young, cutting-edge analyst. A genius. He says so," she wheedled.

"Really?" Joel couldn't hide the delight in his voice. His own dad had never been in the picture. Victor Hodge was everything he aspired to be, a successful Black leader in the community, a family man, a businessman, an outspoken man, a shrewd man. Victor Hodge was one step below Jesus.

Jesus didn't have any daughters to get in the way of their relationship.

"I'm flattered, but—"

The petulance was replaced with obvious impatience. "You're being groomed for junior partner! Don't you get that? Why else would he want you on the ground in London, his personal eyes and ears!" Her hands tugged on the lapels of the button-down shirt he still hadn't shed, even at ten on a Thursday night.

He blinked. "Why would he?"

Vanessa took her hands off of him slowly. With a flustered look, she tucked her hair behind her ear and started gathering the empty paper boxes.

"Vanessa? Why would he?"

"Oh, come on, Joel." She turned to him with a sigh. "Daddy's no fool. He wants to keep the business in the family. Business— well, this kind of business—isn't my thing. A son-in-law in the firm..."

"Son-in-law?" Joel sat down heavily. He knew his tone was stunned and was probably rude, but that didn't matter to him right now. Son-in-law? He'd never even told Vanessa he loved her. He didn't love her, but he liked her and respected her. "Vanessa, I like you a lot. I know on Valentine's Day we... did things."

"We made love. We've made love since, too."

Three times. Each time, he felt his instincts screaming at him to stop and his cock and his intoxicated brain giving in to a beautiful, powerful, sexy woman who told him he was an Adonis, an African god, an answer to her prayers.

"I'm not ready to get married."

"Well, we don't have to right away! But it's been months, Joel. Any mature man, any man who's not just playing with my affections, who's not just *toying* with his *boss's daughter*—" she sliced the words off and sent the daggers into him, "would be thinking about our *future*. I'm almost thirty. You and I—we get things done. I'm goal-oriented. You're a hustler. We are *the* freaking power couple!" She took his hands in hers, the softness returning to her sensuous lips and her hypnotic green eyes. "I'm getting engaged by the end of this year. You're going to London. You, Joel Martin-Hodge, are about to be the international face of Hodge, Williams, and Henderson."

Alarm bells were ringing.

His ego was shouting.

Vanessa was still talking, her mouth moving with seducing whispers alternating with fierce entreaties.

All he wanted was a quiet place to go.

Without warning, he remembered Saturday mornings with Amanda. They would be at his house, studying in silence. His mother was still sleeping, having finished her shift at the hospital at eleven and not falling into bed until after midnight, or else just returning at seven and heading straight for a shower and bed. He and Amanda would make oatmeal and frozen waffles, three plates, one for A.J. who never appeared before ten.

He got so much done. He could think so clearly. Being with Amanda had been as comfortable as being with his own shadow.

The peaceful vision shattered as his world tipped. How was he on his back? Oh, yeah. The coffee table was between him and his couch, but Vanessa didn't seem to notice how close the back of his knees were to it until he was sprawling across it with a groan.

"Oh!" she gasped, both hands to her lips in apology. "I'm so sorry."

"It's okay. It's fine. I'll just have to sleep on my side," he groaned, standing up slowly. "Why don't you get changed and I'll get an aspirin?"

Staring at him uncertainly, she moved back to his bedroom and closed the door.

Joel let out a sigh of relief. *See, man, you should not feel that way about your woman leaving.*

I don't think she's my woman. I might be her man, but it's not mutual. If she were really my woman, I should be able to discuss anything with her. She wants what I don't— at least not right now. Not by the end of the year. Even if I did want to get married right away, I don't want to move. Not across an ocean from Mom. That'd break her heart. Does that make me a Mama's Boy?

His head hurt, his back hurt, his heart hurt.

I want to talk to Amanda.

Amanda's not who you're in trouble with.

"Vanessa?" Joel approached her slowly as she returned, fully dressed, her purse over her arm.

"What, honey?"

"I don't want to live in London. I didn't even know about this idea."

She giggled guiltily, but the mirth didn't reach her eyes. "I wasn't supposed to say anything until after you met with Daddy and had the phone conference tomorrow morning. He wasn't sure how you'd feel about it, but I told him you'd *love* the idea."

"But I don't. I don't love it. I wouldn't mind traveling there, maybe even staying there for a few months, but living there? No."

"You know Daddy sent me to school in Paris? And my mother's sister lives in London. We'd have family there."

"*You* would. My mother and my aunts are here. My brother is here. Aman— And that's not fair for me to leave them." Joel hastily dropped Amanda's name from the list and hoped Vanessa hadn't noticed.

Vanessa noticed everything, everything she *wanted* to see. "Your mom is what—sixty?"

"Fifty-five!" Joel corrected automatically.

"In a few years she'll be in a nursing home."

"What? One, that's crazy. Two, that's all the more the reason not to move away, because she'd need me more than ever. Three, your father is sixty and he's like the Hulk in a hand-cut suit! What the hell do you mean, she'll be in a nursing home!?"

"Don't you dare—" Vanessa's eyes went from hypnotic to nuclear. Anger made her ugly and she knew it. She instantly settled her tone and her features, giving him a frosty smile. "You know what? You're cranky. You haven't eaten, you're working too hard, it's late, and your back hurts. Daddy was right, he should have told you first." Suddenly as sweet as she had been furious, she kissed his cheek and stepped into the hallway. "After a good night's sleep and your meeting tomorrow, you'll be fine. We'll talk tomorrow afternoon."

She left before he could reply.

Instead of feeling excited for his big meeting or looking forward to an enjoyable date, he felt lead in the pit of his stomach. The feeling was akin to watching a merger blow up in his face or hearing that A.J. had indeed lost his scholarship and his chance to play professionally.

He kicked the coffee table and watched the top splinter.

"Splintering. Shattering. Like my future, probably. Amanda loves a good metaphor."

Tomorrow, he was going to call her.

Chapter Four

"**Y**ou've reached Amanda Gardella, Assistant Librarian at Haven University Library. If I didn't answer my phone, I'm probably reading and can't come out of my fictional universe right now. If this is an after hours emergency involving the library, call the Haven University Campus Police at—"

Joel grinned like a fool. Only Amanda would mention books in her voice mail greeting. He almost put the phone down, but her voice, soothing and friendly, was still rolling. "If you need to reach me regarding library business between the hours of 8:00 AM and 5:00 PM, Monday through Friday, please call the Haven University Library's main desk at 888-555-2665 and ask for Amanda Gardella."

"RHONDA, IF A MAN CALLS and asks for me today, tell him—tell him I can't be reached. If he asks for Amanda, just tell him I'm sick."

"You want me to lie?"

"Oh. No. Sorry, unethical. Tell him I'm in an urgent meeting with the periodicals staff."

"But— *you're* the periodicals staff."

"Right, so if you hear me talking to myself, don't interrupt the meeting." Amanda walked away briskly before Rhonda could question her mental health. She knew it was cowardly, but if Robert called today, she couldn't deal with it. She felt guilty. She felt vulnerable. She felt... like her sister probably felt, which totally sucked.

"I can't be with you right now, Robert. It's not your fault. It's not the age difference. It's not you, it's me—which is the worst cliche in the whole world, so why is it true?" she muttered.

"Books?"

Amanda turned with a puzzled frown toward the sound of Rhonda's voice.

"Books here?"

"Only several thousand! What in the world are you—"

"Shh!" Rhonda hushed her, holding the phone to her chest and looking around the largely empty library. Only the hardcore students and faculty were there over Haven's Spring Break. "Is there someone named Books here! I have a phone call for Books from—"

Amanda dropped the stack of *Neuropsychology Today* periodicals she'd been sorting. "From Suits," she mouthed, eyes wide.

"A call from Suits, looking for Books?"

Rhonda had no idea why Amanda grabbed the phone, made a noise like a strangled chicken, and then ran into her tiny cubby of an office. "Uh—you'll take the call? Okay? Amanda?"

"JOEL?" HER VOICE WAS quivering. Amanda couldn't believe that his voice would be the one on the end of the line.

"I asked for Amanda two times and they said you couldn't be disturbed. But it's an emergency, so I took a chance and called again."

"I'm avoiding a phone call from someone. Silly, but true."

"The truth. It's amazing to hear your voice. A-maz-ing."

"You, too!"

Silence. Contentment. Neither one bothered to lay the blame. Both of them had gone from weekly visits once he moved to the city to a few times a year, to texts and calls that decreased in frequency. They exchanged Christmas cards with gift cards inside this past December, but that was it. It was too painful to diagnose the disease that was killing something that had lasted over a decade.

Too different?

He's a guy. I'm a girl.

She's white, I'm African American.

He went to the business side of the world. I stayed in academia by extension.

Silent musings gave way to one shared thought. *None of that matters now.*

"What's the emergency? Are you okay?" Amanda demanded, worry in her voice.

"Avoiding a phone call? Is someone bothering you, 'Manda?" The protective anxiety in Joel's tone was loud and clear.

His heart throbbed in relief.

Hers fluttered in a new and unfamiliar way.

"I think I'm about to make a huge mistake no matter what I do." Joel paused at a busy intersection and watched cars screaming past. The last three years had been set on fast forward. Amanda's next words were like the universe hitting the pause button.

"Why don't you come home?"

JOEL CALLED THE OFFICE from his car, already heading out of the city. "I'm afraid my back started to bother me again." It was semi-true and the truth felt like a heavy-duty painkiller. It loosened his tongue and relaxed his muscles. "I also enjoyed talking to Ralph, Kenneth, and Vish. They seem like awesome guys. I'm open to discussing the London branch, Mr. Hodge. I don't think the company should put someone with my experience level in *charge*, however. I don't have enough knowledge of international laws and liabilities yet."

Mr. Hodge let out a heavy sounding sigh, as if he'd been holding his breath. "That's very wise. I know Vanessa was sure you'd be gung ho about this chance."

"Vanessa is an amazing person." That seemed like the safest thing to say for now. "I'm going to go see my mother this afternoon."

"Yes, right. She's the emergency medicine nurse?"

"My back isn't as bad as all of that. Still, it wouldn't hurt to see her." It had been way too long since he'd gone home for the weekend.

After he hung up, his fingers itched to dial Amanda again. Or Vanessa. He kept his hands locked on the wheel, unwilling to make any more mistakes.

JOEL HAD BEEN TO HER apartment a few times, just after she'd gotten it, when they still made time to visit, each time shorter and farther from the last. Amanda knew it would take him about an hour, maybe more, to get from the city to Haven. She worked through her lunch hour and left Rhonda manning the front desk of the nearly-empty library.

She paced. She put away a book here and there. She washed the coffee cup she'd left on the table. "Should I change?" she asked the silent one-bedroom apartment.

No. No, she wouldn't dress up or dress down for Joel. Her best friend was coming back. She didn't mean simply coming home, she meant that something in Joel was returning. She doubted he would shed his high-powered city-dweller lifestyle, but maybe he was starting to realize the same thing she had.

Suits and Books—they're both full of individuals. Sometimes they work together just fine, even if their coverings are different.

"Amanda?"

Joel's soft voice accompanied his light rapping on the apartment door. She jumped and took a shuddering breath in, throat too tight to give a greeting. Instead, she ripped the door open and stared, her mouth half-open.

Joel rushed in and swooped her up in a bear hug.

Amanda clung to him and squealed as they whirled in the entryway of her apartment. "Oh, my God! You idiot! Never leave for that long again!" She slapped his arm when he put her down, then hugged him again.

"I won't. I won't." There was a ring of quiet conviction in his voice. "Wow." Joel pushed her to arm's length, smoothing her copper and blonde hair from her face.

"What?" Amanda regarded him with a half-smile.

"Being around you straightens out my head, girl." He slung his suit jacket off and dropped it over the back of her kitchen chair.

"That's good." She gave him a tiny grin. "So, wanna tell me about the big mistakes I'm about to save you from?"

"SO, LEMME GET THIS straight." Amanda swallowed the last bite of the frozen pizza they were sharing. "You think if you dump Vanessa, you might lose your job?"

"Yeah."

"But if you don't go to London and you don't propose, she might dump you?"

"Then her dad might fire me, because I broke his only daughter's heart." He untucked the napkin he'd placed over his shirt front. "Damn it." One splotch of grease evaded the napkin. Joel wiped his fingers and began unbuttoning the shirt.

"Like prom night all over again," Amanda mused aloud.

"Huh?" Joel looked up, shirt sliding down over his shoulders.

She was momentarily speechless. Her friend had filled out, his biceps were larger, his abs standing out under the clinging white ribbed cotton of his undershirt, and the almost-manicured look of his stubbled face only brought out the width of his perfect jaw.

"You got prettier." Amanda's brain apparently left the filter off.

He chuckled. "Well, you would know." Amanda was wearing a belted olive dress, black leggings and bare feet. Her hair still didn't want to stay up or back and her cat's eye glasses magnified her warm eyes ever so slightly. "You didn't change a bit."

Amanda frowned. "How does that make any sense? *I* said you got prettier and *you*—"

"You were always so perfect lookin', so gorgeous. You look even better now. Haven't seen you in so long," he admitted, shaking his head.

Her cheeks felt decidedly hot. In fact, other places felt hot, too. It's just Joel, just Joel, just Joel, her brain soothed.

Screw that.

"I don't like Vanessa. She sounds manipulative. You're not comfortable around her if you're afraid that you'll end up losing your job just for being honest. A person who really loves you would understand if you said, 'Look, I don't want to leave my whole life and move to a foreign country. Plus, I don't think it's wise for the company.' Or, if you said, 'Look, I don't think I'm ready to get married yet.' Even if she was mad, even if she didn't like it, if she respects you and cares about you she'd listen!" Amanda flung her hands up. Joel stared at her intently, unspeaking. "What? Is there pepperoni in my teeth?"

"No." Joel shook his head slowly. "She doesn't."

"She doesn't? Or I don't?"

"She doesn't respect me. She might *care* about me. I don't know if she loves me. She loves what we could do together. We could be a power couple. She's been 'groomed' her whole life to be the power behind the throne, the wealthy businessman's wife, a shareholder, or something." Joel pushed his chair back. "I'm starting to wonder if any hot, smart guy in good with her dad's company would have suited her. Oh, man...." His fingers raked over the close-cropped curls, head tilted back to lean wearily on the sunburnt pink of her living room wall. "I got played and I didn't realize it."

"You didn't get played! You met someone you thought you could make it work with. That's all we're trying to do, all of us are just trying to make it work. Find someone to love." Amanda gave a hopeless shrug.

Joel pounced. "Personal experience?"

Amanda hesitated. Why did admitting to seeing Robert make her stomach squirm guiltily? "Not really. I was dating someone I met *at* work, but not a co-worker. We went out, kind of casually. I really liked him. We had fun together. He wanted to move things along, take things up a level, and I couldn't do that. I wasn't in love with him. That's the bottom line, in 'Suits' lingo."

"Or if I'm speaking in 'Books', that's all she wrote?" he countered.

"All she wrote," Amanda agreed, coming to stand beside him. "So. What do you think you should do?"

WHY WAS AMANDA'S NEARNESS suddenly making his thoughts fuzzy? With Vanessa, she had been quick to introduce him to the good wines he'd never experienced, expensive Scotch, even brandy and port, which he found too rich and cloying. He found himself feeling heavy and off-balance. Hearing Amanda's voice had made him feel free and light after months in a concrete prison.

"Joel?" Amanda backed up slightly.

Joel fixed her with a burning gaze, somehow a cross between the hard, hungry stare that had once alarmed his best friends and the warm friendliness he'd missed sharing with her.

This kind of "fuzzy" was warm and safe, like waking up from a good dream. "I'm going to ask her out."

"Vanessa?" Amanda squawked

Joel snickered. Amanda was about one step from smacking him for his own good. "No. The girl I love. Amanda."

"What?"

"Amanda, do you wanna go out with me?" His lips twitched, trying not to laugh at her flabbergasted expression.

Joel waited for her response, but Amanda seemed to be fixated on his lips. He waited for a moment. As she remained silent, his smile faded, replaced by the nervous look he used to get as the shot clock ticked down when his team needed one more basket to win.

"Oh! Did you— did you ask me that for real?" Amanda finally blurted.

Joel nodded, his ego instantly bruised. She thought it was a joke?

"YES! Oh my gosh, *yes*! Yes, I would love to!"

A relieved laugh bubbled up from his lips. "Really?"

"Yes! Duh!" Amanda flung her arms around Joel's neck and laughed into the hollow of his shoulder.

"Oh, Babe! Are you crying?" Joel tilted her chin up as she struggled to shake it free. "Well, look. I promise you— I promise you I'm not going to make you cry ever again unless it's happy tears. Deal?" His thumbs traced the tears away, impulsively followed by his lips. When he got close, his lips on her skin, he couldn't help but inhale, pulling the scent of her deep into his lungs. Vanilla and cinnamon. Good enough to eat. His lips pressed a few more unnecessary kisses to her cheeks, waiting for her to pull away.

She was gasping softly against him, turning her head to let her lips meet his. "These are happy tears," she explained between soft, chaste kisses.

"Ohh, 'Manda. Missed you." He'd never kissed her before, not like this. How did this feel so perfect and familiar? The times with Vanessa had felt hurried or too dragged out, but this— he felt everything flowing easily between them. If it ended right now, he'd long for more. If it kept going, he'd be content.

"I think about you all the time."

"Like this?" His lips were working slowly over the other side of her face now, bowing his head low, cupping her cheeks with both hands to lift her face higher.

"Well... maybe a little bit. I started realizing that the more I was with other guys, I would really rather—"

"—be with you." Joel finished her thought, which was his as well. Amanda's fingers were digging into his shoulders, her lips finding his again. "Damn, girl...."

AMANDA LOVED THE SATINY feel of his soft skin under her cheek, smelling of cocoa butter and blended citrus and spice. *He's home. He's here. Home. In my arms.* His appreciative, breathless, "Damn, girl..." jolted her out of her mental cocoon for a moment. Was she doing too much? Too soon? She'd been hesitant to do more than even kiss Robert, but her body had no such compunctions with Joel. Her hips squirmed forward, meeting his as they bumped against the wall. "Did you ever think of me? Like this?" she asked against her better judgement. What if he said no?

"Nuh-uh. Thought of you even better."

Their bodies, blocked by the wall, seemed to have figured out that if they couldn't go through, they'd best keep moving to the side. Thumping and spinning like an unbalanced wheel, they found themselves exiting the living room and ending up in her room.

This wasn't something new. Joel had been in literally every bedroom she ever had, even this one. He'd sat on every bed. This time, they stopped at the foot of it, their lips parting with a surprised gasp.

"What are we doing?" Joel panted.

"Homecoming?" Amanda suggested. *Wait, what* am *I doing? He still has a girlfriend, technically. I just broke up. Am I on the rebound? Is he cheating on her if he's planning to break up?*

"You *are* home. My home. You and Mom and A.J. You mean home to me. You mean more than everything I ever worked for, you know that?" he told her fervently, his hands tight on her soft, slender arms. "I'd trade all the money, all the mergers and meetings, all the suits in the world for you to be my girl."

"You don't have to trade. You can have us both. Books and Suits. They go together. They can, if we work at it. I'll work so hard, Joel. I got that job as librarian when you didn't think I—"

"Hush that talk. That was some stupid young ass talking. He doesn't live here anymore. You always work hard and you get what you want. You're my hustle."

"Because I know you, that's like the sweetest thing ever. Now my eyes are leaking again." Amanda wiped her wrist across her damp lids before returning her arms to around his neck. "Whenever you and I hug for too long, like this," she paused as his hands rested on her hips and they swayed to a song only the two of them could hear, the last slow dance song from senior prom, "I get teary."

"Does that mean I should stop?" he murmured, forehead to hers.

"Nope. Means you'd better keep doing it. I only cry 'cause I think we're going to have to let go."

"Let me show you how I can hold onto you, Books." His hands skimmed down further, cupping her round rear.

Amanda approved, snuggling her pelvis to him, her eyes widening. "Oh!" Holy crap. Joel was hard. Hard and big. She could feel him through his perfectly creased trousers. The thought didn't fill her with anxiety as thoughts of sleeping with Robert had. "That's a good thing. We want this. I mean, *I* want this. Not as some rebound thing, but as a real thing. A permanent thing. I know you're not ready to get married. I'm not ready to get married! I meant—ugh."

"I get you, Books. You mean the main characters get the happily ever after?"

"Yes, but if you call me Cinderella, I reserve the right to spill stuff on your precious silk ties, Suits."

Kissing through their laughter, Amanda tentatively reached forward and let her hands find the hem of his thin undershirt and roll it up. Her breathing was fast and uneven as Joel's deft fingers started undoing the buttons on her dress, then shifted to the belt.

"We don't have to do this now. We didn't go out. I asked you out," he blurted as his hands prepared to slide under the newly-loosened fabric and push the dress to the floor.

"I'd rather stay in. We had pizza. Later we could have a movie."

"Later, I could give you your own private show," he teased.

"Oooh, I bet." Which brought another thought to mind. Was Joel going to care that this was her first time? He'd *care*, obviously, he was her best friend, about to become her lover, but would it seem odd since he'd started having sexual experiences while she'd been stubbornly waiting to feel the Big L?

"This is the first time. We should make this special. It is special! Because it's you and me, but— Vanessa and I went to a ski resort. I could take you someplace. I'd take you anyplace. Where you wanna go, Baby?"

"To bed. With you."

"Awww, damn. This is why I love you. Why I'm in love with you. Girl, I think I've been in love with you my whole life. I was just too stubborn to notice."

"Ditto. We liked proving that boys and girls could keep it platonic. We defied the rumor mill. Um. Sort of."

"Hey, we did it, until we wised up. Now we're breaking another 'rule.'" He kissed her neck until she moaned and tilted her head back into his palm, letting him get better access, letting him nuzzle the olive fabric down and reveal a sheer black bra that only highlighted the creamy color of her skin. "You and I are about to smash out of the Friend Zone."

"Smash seems a little hard," Amanda sighed, her fingers dipping over the hard lines of his muscles until they reached his belt. Boldly, she let them trace the contours of his cock through the layers of fabric. "Your turn to gasp," she whispered as his head rolled back.

"You take me out of the world. Didn't even need a plane ticket."

Amanda smiled at his dazed voice. Now in nothing but a bra and skin-tight black leggings, she was undoing his belt as she kissed his chest, gently slipping her tongue back and forth across one nipple. His enthusiastic noises convinced her that her actions up top must have a direct link to his cock.

"Ohhh, fuck. Where'd you learn that?" Joel hissed as his pants slid down, leaving him in nothing but socks and burgundy boxer briefs.

"Books." *Okay, yes. You should tell him. In case it matters at some point, or in case it hurts and you need him to help you, you should tell him.* "I'm entirely book taught. Aside from some pretty hefty kisses, this is the farthest I've gone. Our first time *is* my first time."

She loved the look of admiring pride on his face as he murmured, "You wanted true love. Accept no substitutes. You do anything you put your mind to, girl. Well, I'm gonna try to make any dream you've got come tr—ow. Oww."

Amanda, who'd been reveling in the fairytale moment of Joel literally sweeping her off her feet, almost crashed back to earth. His face was twisted in pain and he grabbed for his shoulder as soon as she was free of his arms.

"Joel! What happened? What's wrong?" She hunched down, lifting him up as he was doubling over. "Too much pizza?"

"I hurt my back last night; tripped backwards and landed on my coffee table. Caught the sharp corner with my shoulder."

The roles were now reversed and they were both okay with that. Who said the princess couldn't also be a strong woman, nestling the injured knight onto her bed? She slid a pillow under his shoulder as concern bloomed on her face.

She watched his face relax as the pain ebbed away. "Not *too* sore, though," he hinted.

"Goody," Amanda breathed, kneeling beside him. Her breath caught as his lips nuzzled her breast through the sheer cup, as his hand slowly reached back and touched the hooks that held it on. "You can."

He swallowed. "Don't want you to think badly about me, but—"

"I promise I don't! We weren't together so whatever we did or didn't do isn't a guilt thing. Okay?"

He relaxed slightly. "I wasn't that great with Vanessa. I wasn't comfortable, so my head wasn't in the game. I was *good* enough, y'know, according to her, but," he shrugged self-consciously, eyes timidly seeking her amused smile, "this is a first for me, too. First time it's love, not just sex."

"Mm. See, I think we were waiting for each other."

"Mm-hmm. And I think I like the way you think."

"I also think you'd feel better if you finish one chapter before moving onto the next." Amanda pulled back slightly as the trousers on the floor made a soft buzzing sound.

"Smart girl." He sighed and kissed her. "Hold that thought?"

Chapter Five

"Daddy told me you refused the job in London! *Refused*!" Vanessa's irate voice made him recoil.

I am a strong, smart man. I'm not some boy that you picked up off the street and made into a success. I am a success. When he spoke aloud, his voice was steady. "Technically, I didn't get a firm offer, but I don't know why you're so surprised. I told you I didn't want to move there. I was very clear about that."

"Joel! This is our chance! This is—"

"Vanessa, why can't this be *your* chance? Why don't you go over there and be his eyes and ears? You grew up in boardrooms. You have a bachelor's in marketing, right? Go back to school and—"

Her harsh laugh froze his words. "No. No, no, no. You don't get to dictate to me."

"You don't get to dictate to me, either."

"I'm not dictating, I'm helping you! I'm *gifting* you! I'm Vanessa Hodge, I'm incredibly influential in the company that you claim to love. Are you trying to get yourself demoted? Fired?"

He smiled, shaking his head slowly. How had he ever thought this relationship was right, that it was even mutual? How had he not realized before that he wasn't really a love interest, more like collateral interest? "I know that you're angry."

"Of course I'm angry! You're throwing everything away!"

"I'm not quitting my job! But I'm not ready to go head up some international office and I'm not ready to get married. I'm not what you're looking for. I'm sorry I didn't realize it until last night."

Shocked silence greeted his words. "Are you... dumping me?"

"I'd like to think we're both smart enough to realize that we're not a good fit. We want different things—or at least, we want them at different speeds. Is that fair to say?" He kept his cool with an effort, even as he felt his career starting a death swirl down the proverbial toilet.

"Of course, it's not fair to say! Again, a man ruins a woman's aspirations and says that it's all for the best."

His chuckle was bitter, loud enough for Vanessa to hear. "Your aspirations included me, included me in ways I didn't want. I might even say you used me, but I didn't ever feel used until you made it clear that you weren't listening to me. That's probably not fair to either of us, but you were right about something. We could be a power couple. We are smart, strong people. Stubborn people. We didn't see that we were pulling in two different directions this whole time, 'Nessa. I think you're one half of a power couple, and I'm one half. We just aren't the whole. You need—"

"Don't you presume to tell me what *I* need. I need a real man. Not some boy playing in his daddy's suits."

"Don't know my daddy. Don't know if he wore suits. My son is gonna know exactly who his father is and how he got shit done. Whether I get it done working *for* Hodge, Williams, and Henderson or for some *other* firm, that won't matter to him. I'd hate to leave such a great company, but if your dad fires me 'cause we break up? Hey. Sometimes the game is played behind the scenes. Politics. Backrooms. Bedrooms." He shrugged with an apathy he didn't really feel. "Pretty sure Victor Hodge has more honor than that. I guess we'll see."

Vanessa sputtered something. Joel felt his heart twist as he realized that under the angry little mutters, she was crying. "I'm sorry. I'm sorry I didn't know sooner."

"I want the couch back."

He tilted his head. Of all the things he'd expected her to say, that wasn't it. "Okay. I'm looking to move closer to home. Do you want to pick it up Sunday or Monday?"

"I—you're impossible."

Amanda, sitting on the far side of the bed with her knees to her chest and worried eyes, gave him a tiny smile.

Yes, it *was* impossible. There was no way in hell he belonged with Vanessa Hodge. His heart firmly belonged to the sexy librarian on the edge of the bed. "If you want to talk more when you come and get the couch, we can."

"I have nothing more to say to you, Joel. If you can't see what you're missing, I'm not standing around to let you get a better look! I'll text you when I'm sending someone over to pick it up."

Before he could say goodbye, she hung up. Joel fell back, ignoring the stabbing throb in his shoulder. In seconds, soft, honey-colored hair tickled his cheek. Amanda's head was next to his, her fingers weaving with his own.

"I thought you said a difficult thing the best way you could. Of course, I'm highly biased in favor of what you said. Your son, if you ever have one, is going to know that you did this all on your own."

"Nah. I did it with some help. Couldn't be such a smart man without my Books. You see what I did there?"

He smiled as Amanda rolled her eyes. "I see what you did there. That was tough, though. Do you need to call Mr. Hodge? Maybe you two need to figure out what happens next?" She didn't want to say, "If you're fired or not."

"I care what happens at work, but for the first time in a long time, I want to focus on something else. What happens next *here*. Between us." He rolled to his side, taking in the angelic face and the hills of cleavage that were all pressed up, the soft, undefined middle above her perfectly grabbable hips.

"First, I get rid of these." Amanda methodically took off her glasses and put them on her bedside table.

"Ohhh, it's about to get real. The glasses came off," he chuckled, snuggling deeper into her soft bed with a feeling of contentment in his heart and excitement in his hips.

"This girl means business. I've been waiting for three years to break you out of that prison you call an office."

"It's not a prison!" He did love his job.

Amanda sat up and put her hands on her hips. The effect was adorable, especially as her hair flopped crazily over one eye. "If they only let you out for fresh air once a day, it's a prison."

"I promise to improve my work-life balance, Beautiful. Did you happen to catch that part where I said I was looking for a place closer to home?"

Her lips buzzed across his as she made a noise of agreement. "Your mom has two empty rooms, you know."

"I was hoping it would be a place halfway between the university library and my office. Y'know, so we'd both have to commute about the same distance."

"Me? Commute?"

"If you want to. What I meant was— I was thinking that I—damn." He'd just told Vanessa he wasn't ready to get serious and five minutes later, he wanted to go apartment hunting with Amanda? "Too fast?"

Amanda's lips pursed as her hands ran down his chest. "Maybe. It sounds just like something you would do. Making a good investment? Calculating trends and future returns?" Her lips framed the words and dragged them out, her tongue flickering over her top lip as she concluded.

Joel had never realized hearing Amanda say words that related to his passion would make them seem incredibly sexy. The throbbing in his shoulder moved abruptly to his groin. "You're in my future, aren't you?"

"Exactly."

He was practically salivating, watching her move, listening to her talk. The girl was working him over like he tore through date, her eyes raking over him in a blend of shyness and seduction. He knew his chest was rising and falling like he'd run a marathon, and she hadn't even done much more than speak.

"Wanna invest in me, Baby?" Amanda purred.

That woman. She knew exactly which buttons to push, and he loved her for it! "Ohh, God yes." He ran his hand possessively up her arms, pulling her to his chest.

"I promise it has high yields." Her lips danced over his throat.

"Stop, you temptress." He bit her lobe softly, making her squeal and arch into him. "Oh, fuck, Amanda... You're going to make it hard to take my time."

"If it's only the one time?" she led.

"Nope. No, no, lots and lots of times. As long as you want me."

Her eyes met his. "I've *always* wanted you in my life. I don't know when the roles changed. No, not changed. You're still my best friend."

"I'm glad I'm gonna be more."

HER HAND STROKED DOWN his chest and met the stretchy soft fabric covering the impressive bulge. His hands mirrored hers, undoing her bra and pressing reverent kisses to her breasts, capturing a nipple and tonguing it slowly until she whimpered and guided his hand to her thigh.

They shifted together, her leggings and her panties rolling off as one, down her shapely calves and over her ankles. He nudged his socks down as she inhaled sharply, scooping his cock out of its confines. "Wow. Wow." She stroked up and down, fingers twirling briefly in the coarse patch above his manhood.

"I was thinking the same thing."

Amanda's breath caught as Joel massaged her plump backside and raked gently over her golden-brown curls. She shifted as she laid on her back, changing his hand's position to slip between her legs, going where no one had ever touched her.

His tone was almost reverent. "You're so soft."

"Well, you're so hard," she laughed. She'd experimented in pleasuring herself; she was twenty-five after all. She hadn't done more than rub herself to orgasm, sometimes testing the sensation of a finger or two moving in and out. It never felt as good as she thought it should.

"I'll go nice and slow. Won't feel hard," he promised, something like worry in his eyes.

"It's you and me. I'm not worried. You don't have to do the, 'I'll be gentle' speech."

Joel frowned. "But I will be, 'cause I love you."

She beamed and moved against his hand. "I know, that's why I'm not worried."

HIS HAND EXPLORED AS they kissed, squeezing one breast. They were so soft, round, and way more delectable-looking than he'd realized all those years at the beach. Down to stroke her curls, down to find her so soft and wet, not to mention the perfect shade of dewy tulip pink. Like— how could you not want that in your mouth? Resisting kissing it would defy the laws of science. Analysts were very scientific people.

"Oh, Joel. Wha...?" Amanda sounded surprised at the loss of his lips.

"I didn't do this yet, but I think I can figure it out." He knelt beside her knees.

"Not a math problem. Oh! Oh, God!"

Joel knew Amanda hated the predatory side him, but perhaps he could convince her that in this one area, it was beneficial. His tongue swept across the seam of her nether lips and tapped hard on her clit. Whatever he did must have been good. Her hips bucked under his hands and her fingers clutched his short, sleek hair.

"Mmmm. You're yummy. So pretty, too. Damn, seriously, why'd God put the prettiest parts on the inside? Look how pink you are!" Joel lifted his head to reflect on the mysteries of the universe and then dove back down to lap at her sweet pussy, spreading her lips and enjoying her bucking hips that made him twist and turn to keep up with her.

"I don't know," she half-whimpered.

Joel gently slid one finger inside of her while he began a steady sucking on her clit. He moved slowly in and out while the tempo of his lips increased. His mouth and hands went seeking and exploring until the knot of pressure inside her unraveled. Her fingers scraped the nape of his neck as she screamed softly.

He was beside her in a second, holding her tight. "Oh, Baby! 'Manda I'm sorry, so sorry. You felt wet enough, I'm sorry."

"Shut up, you made me cum. Whoo. Even my toes are all tingly," she panted, hugging him back. "I never—no one ever made me cum. Intense. But a very good kind of intense!"

His shoulders sagged in relief. "I thought I poked something inside."

"You felt good inside. Can't wait for more."

"Well, then." He began to roll atop of her, only to find her hands pushing him flat. "Wanna be on top?"

"Wanna return the favor."

His girl pulled herself to unsteady knees and scooted down the rumpled bed. Joel's cock was hard and filled her curled palm. While she stroked, he moaned, eyes struggling to stay open and watch her. She looked adorable as she studied him, like finding a particularly delightful passage in a book. Finally, she turned her body so that her head was over his waist and her legs were up by his torso. She gently kissed the tip of his dark, reddish-brown member, slowly sliding her tongue over the tip and closing her eyes.

"Oh. Sweet. Jesus." Joel's jaw dropped and stayed down. Amanda was giving him every fantasy he'd ever had, not just about her, but about anyone. She was into it, into him, finding his hand and holding it, turning again to squat between his legs so that their eyes met as she took him deeper and deeper into her mouth. He stroked her hair and let his fingertips gently follow the curves of her face. How you could feel this hot and this holy all at once was a mystery. *This is what it must be like- to make love with the person you've been waiting for. Your other half.* "I love you."

She dragged her tongue up the large vein in his cock once more and ended with a hard suck over his sensitive tip. "I love you, too. I was going to do more of that."

"I want you to wait. I wanna be inside of you. If you're ready? We'll go slow."

"Nuh-uh, we'll go at Joel-and-Amanda-speed. We arrive just when we're supposed to."

Her utter faith in him made his eyes prickle. "Girl, don't you make me tear up right now."

She shrugged. "We'll say it's sweat."

"Someone's planning to give me a workout, huh?"

"I've got months of fantasies about you, Joel Martin. You have some serious work to do."

FEELING HIM ON TOP of her was the best feeling, sex and safety, rolled into one. His mouth met hers as his fingers were busy, feeling her out, thrusting one, then two, until she couldn't take it anymore. "I want you inside me. I want to feel you in, all the way in," Amanda hissed into his shoulder. Truthfully, she wasn't sure if he'd fit in all the way. From her reading, she knew the vagina lengthened when aroused. She was more turned-on than she'd ever been in her entire life so she assumed he'd have no trouble.

Amanda knew Joel was a patient guy. He'd worked hard to get everything he had. Right now, she could see form the intensity on his face that he was struggling to keep that patience. She could relate. She wanted all of him inside of her, right now. Instead, they were still working up to it, with his hand between their bodies, his thumb on her clit, making her moan his name in an endless loop.

Joel moaned back. "I dream about you calling my name like that. Talking to me when I'm inside you."

"I want you so bad." Her hand snaked down past his and gripped his cock, slippery from rubbing against her without going inside. Her hips opened and he instinctively moved down a little as she bucked up, suddenly connecting, sinking into her as she shuddered pleasurably.

Okay, so he was a lot bigger than her two fingers, but he was also capable of hitting some spot that she'd always missed. "Hold still," she hissed, hugging him tight.

"All night, right here." He kissed her forehead. "Honey—"

"Shhh. It's a little tight."

"Understatement of the century," he grunted back.

Her pussy was fluttering and squeezing like it wanted to pull Joel in deeper and hadn't quite figured out how. She could tell he was holding still until she started to move, but when her hips bumped his, the waiting was over. They rocked as one, slotting together until there was no space left between them.

Amanda felt a cramping sensation that settled into bliss within moments. Joel's thickness was filling her up completely, putting pressure on all the internal spots that craved attention.

"Good?" he whispered.

"So good."

"I'm so glad I came home. Came home to my girl." He buried his head on the pillow, neck craned.

She rubbed his shoulders, hands reaching down to sink into his cheeks and pull him in tight. As she let the tempo of her hips increase, he matched her, perfectly in sync.

"Oh. Oh, wow, that's *good*. *That's* worth waiting for," Amanda gasped.

"Hell, yes!" He grit his teeth. "Oh, *fuck*, yes!"

"Joel! Such a naughty mouth." She bit her lip, eyes twinkling.

He stared at her, unsure if they were playing. For one thing, she'd heard him get in his one and only fender bender in their freshman year of college. He could say a lot worse.

"Feels good?" she licked her lips, flicking his too as her tongue darted out.

"Amazing, sweetheart." His teeth were still grit. "Trying not to—"

"I love that big cock, slipping in and out of my tight little pussy."

"Oh my God. Don't play."

"What, I can't talk dirty to you? It's not dirty if it's the guy you love— sliding his thick cock all the way into me. Can't you feel how much I like it? How wet it makes me?"

"I'm going to cum in you in ten seconds if you keep that up."

"I want your cum in me. Want to feel you pop." Her teeth worried his earlobe as her hand tweaked a nipple.

"I'm going to marry you."

"Well, yeah, but—later, right?" she giggled, heart leaping, ribs tight. *Marry Joel?*

Yes. Absolutely.

"I love you for your brain, and your beauty, and your hot little mouth. Finding out that you're secretly a sex goddess just seals the deal. Where did you learn to—"

"Books, Baby. I'm all about those books." She dug her hands in tighter, urging him on. Her eyes closed and her hips took over, riding, thrusting up, loving the hot, hard pressure of him on her upper wall.

"Girl, I'm coming to book club from now on." His eyes rolled back.

Amanda wasn't surprised. Right now, her pussy was an acrobat, fluttering, crunching, leaking hot juice down her thighs and causing wet slapping sounds as he increased the pace again. His balls hit her split-peach pussy and she wailed, her fingers frantically wriggling past his pelvic bone to find her clit.

"Rub that pretty pearl for me, Baby?"

"It—it just feels so good with both..." she whimpered.

"I want you to feel good, I want you to cum. Then *I'm* gonna cum. Then we're gonna eat popcorn, watch a movie, and do this all over again."

"Ohhh! Oh, Joel, promise me?" She yanked his hand to her pussy and curled his fingers around the soft padding over her mound, wanting him to help rub her to orgasm, feel his hands on her and his cock in her. Her ankles hooked together over the small of his back and her hands hooked together at the base of his neck.

"I promise. I love you. Baby, I'm—"

"Cumming! I'm cumming!" she leaned up to let her forehead catch his lips, feeling his body start shake as her tremors subsided. He groaned, shoulders thrust back, then bowed in, falling to her.

"Hooo," he let out a high-pitched sigh, head drooping onto her soft breast, the sweat of his brow mingling with the dew on her bust.

"Whoa." Amanda agreed. "I love you."

"I love you, too." He looked up at her, happy, panting, and smiling wider than he ever had in his life.

She gave him an identical look. "High five, Suits?" She held up her hand.

He slapped it. "Damn straight, Books."

Epilogue

The next afternoon...

"Hi, Mom."

"Joel!" Renee squealed in shocked delight and hauled her son through the door—only to find it much harder than she expected. The boy seemed to have an anchor trailing behind him. Joel's hand was firmly clasped in Amanda's.

"Amanda told me I need to get my mind off the office, so I'm here for book club," he said, hugging his mother tightly with his free arm. "Oh! Hi, Michelle!" he called as Mrs. Gardella came to the entryway and stopped, blinking in delighted surprise to see her pseudo-son standing before her.

"I also told him that I missed him," Amanda piped up, a sneaky grin spreading from her face to his.

"So, I think the way to solve the problem is to convince her to spend more time with me, but the damn library..."

"That corporate office..." Amanda pretended to huff.

"What's happening?" Renee finally demanded, reaching behind her to clutch Michelle's arm for support.

"We decided we're done being best friends—well, *just* best friends. Mom, I told you I'd bring home the right girl one day." Joel pushed Amanda forward, into his mother's startled arms.

"Mom, you're gonna get that son you've been wanting." Amanda pulled her mother into the hug as well.

In the midst of all the squealing and hugging that followed, no one read a single word. No one gave a damn.

"We're a good team, Baby." Joel pulled Amanda into his lap as their mothers were still jumping and giggling like school girls in the dining room.

"I told you we were the perfect couple."

"You did not!"

"I did, too!"

"Not before yesterday!"

"Shut up and kiss me, Suits."

"Bossy Books. Good thing I love you."

"Mmm. Yes. Yes, it is."

If you enjoyed this tale, I would be so encouraged by a review on Goodreads, Bookbub, or any book retailer website or review site.

Thank you in advance, dear readers!

ABOUT THE AUTHOR

BESTSELLING AND AWARD-winning author S.C. Principale believes in writing stories she wants to read, which is why she writes thrillers, mysteries, and steamy paranormal romances. Her stories are filled with strong, sassy heroines and the unique, often otherworldly men who love them. S.C. lives in historic Chester County, Pennsylvania, where haunted battlegrounds serve as never-ending inspiration. S.C. is a self-proclaimed history nerd, following old mysteries, baking, and leading theater and musical groups. Her home life consists of scrounging space for her laptop without tripping over two kids, two dogs, a mischievous chinchilla, and the most patient, sexy husband in the world. **Visit her website for a free gift!** [1]

scprincipaleauthor@gmail.com
Author Website and Newsletter [2]
Twitter[3]

---

1. https://scprincipale.wixsite.com/website

2. https://scprincipale.wixsite.com/website

Instagram[4]
Facebook[5]
S.C.'s Sultry Sweethearts Facebook Readers Group[6]
Tiktok[7]
Goodreads[8]
Amazon [9]

---

*READ THE NEXT PAGE for an excerpt from
CrossRealms: Healing Hope by S.C. Principale.*

---

3. https://twitter.com/SCPrincipale

4. https://www.instagram.com/s.c.principale/

5. https://www.facebook.com/WritesandBites

6. https://www.facebook.com/groups/66828927695362

7. https://www.tiktok.com/@scprincipaleauthor

8. https://www.goodreads.com/author/show/14847508.S_C_Principale

9. https://www.amazon.com/S.C.-Principale/e/
   B01FZZL28I%3Fref=dbs_a_mng_rwt_scns_share

CROSSREALMS
HEALING HOPE
S.C. PRINCIPALE

SOMETIMES TWO BROKEN people make one whole...

Hope Maguire has always been a loner, both by choice and necessity. She'd learned from a young age not to expect anything from anyone, and that suited her fine. In her line of work, friends would be nothing but liabilities anyway. Most Hunters don't live long, so why get attached? When she's assigned to Malcolm, a stuffy, inexperienced Guardian of the Guild, and then sent to work with the team (ugh!) at the Creek Valley CrossRealms, she's sure it's going to be disastrous.

Self-fulfilling prophecy much?

Approached by a third party and asked to inform on her fellow agents, Hope thinks she's doing the right thing—until it's revealed that she has been a pawn in a deadly double-cross. Now, assassins are after her, and it's run or die. Too bad a near-fatal attack has left her as weak as the prey she used to stalk. Hope knows she is as good as dead. No one will save a Hunter who turned on the good guys. Right?

Malcolm Mansfield-Smythe has always regarded Hunters as tools for killing demons and little else. When his rebellious Hunter betrays them all and then ends up on the chopping block herself, it's tempting to forget about her and keep being the empty, by-the-book man he's always been. Except... he doesn't want to be that hollow automaton anymore, and he doesn't think Hope wants to be a cold-blooded weapon, either. A daring (but poorly planned) rescue leads to a life on the run. Forced to rely only on each other, can two enemies find a way to become friends— or even more?

Healing Hope
Territory

APRIL 2006

"Winters Interventions." Harold Winters picked up the phone at the front desk. Typically, he remained closeted in the back of the agency, but he was currently short-staffed. This investigative agency, which handled paranormal issues as well as the mundane spousal affairs and stolen property, was simply a cover. Oh, his true work dealt with the supernatural as well, but much more intimately.

Harold Winters was a Guardian of the Guild, the secretive and elite group of men and women who possessed the knowledge to train those who could see through the Mists. The Mists cloud most human eyes to the supernatural elements among them.

His receptionist was one such person, and as such, she was out helping on an assignment, tracking down whatever had been terrorizing a rather rundown area of Creek Valley, home of the California CrossRealms, a place where the Heavenly, Earthly, and Hell Realms were separated by only a thin margin.

"It's me," Beryl, the receptionist in question, chirped cheerfully. "Maddox and I killed a big scaly demon by Scarlet's. He was going to ravish me in the back alley, but then he said that might not be a good idea."

"Who, the demon or Maddox?" Winters felt like he had to double-check. His ravishing receptionist was a reverted succubus, after all. Sex was her second nature, a perk for her lucky human fiancee, the stalwart Maddox.

Beryl made a noise of disgust. "Maddox! I'm not into scales. Plus, Celeste and Auggie are here. Also, it's Friday. We haven't had a nice, demon-free evening in weeks. Well, present company excluded."

"I'll pass on the invitation. We *are* rather slammed at the agency, you know." He loved his agents dearly, despite the clear rules that stated Guardians of the Guild should remain firmly detached from them, especially given their startlingly high mortality rate. "I shall stay here and consult with our recently seconded Guardian."

"You two just want to get rid of all the Americans and then drink all the tea and say words like snog and knickers," Beryl huffed. "I don't like Mansfield-Smythe. He's a pompous ass. Not a *lovable* pompous ass like you are. He says Celeste and Auggie shouldn't work together, and Maddox and I can't have sex on my desk. It's *my* desk!"

"Technically it's my desk as I own the premises and all the furnishings, and I happen to agree with him on that point."

"But Maddox says you'd have a stroke if we used *your* desk."

"I am *not* having this conversation."

"I don't like him. He treats us like robots."

Winters pinched the bridge of his nose to stave off the headache he felt surging forth. For a full decade, he'd worked in Guild Headquarters in London. He oversaw a much larger area with many Guardians reporting to him. He regarded all of them with cool, precise detachment. Only a few years in the Creek Valley CrossRealms with a bunch of young upstarts had turned him soft. Oh, he could assist and train his entire team of young Hunters, Warriors, wiccas, and field agents, even associate with the occasional willing Darkling. But five minutes on the phone with Beryl....

She was still talking about Mansfield-Smythe's many faults. "... never goes on field assignments, wants our reports typed and handed in like we're pupils at some freakshow school, never trains in hand-to-hand with us, never even takes his tie off! I think he irons his underwear. And maybe his hair. If you ask me, it's a waste of a cute face and a nice posh accent."

"I did *not* ask you and he's simply doing what other Guardians do, what *most* other Guardians do. *I* am the aberration, not him. Also, he's quite right to recommend that couples do not work in the field together. It can cause distraction and hinder successful missions and investigations."

"You also have way more at stake and you can't let the baddies win. Look, you're old. You have way more experience than he does. This is his first field assignment, right? You teach him! Don't let him corrupt you."

Winters grimaced against the receiver, "My dear, I'm already considered corrupted and irredeemable by most of the Guild. If Felicia hadn't led this team to victory against the dark forces so many times, they'd have stripped me of my rights and titles, my pension and my salary... even my lapel pin."

"Not the sacred lapel pin." Beryl laughed and turned. A strong hand was kneading her shoulder pointedly. "Saving innocent people makes me horny. Maddox, too."

"Dear Lord."

"Just tell everyone who wants to meet at Scarlet's that we'll be waiting for them. In a dark corner behind some potted plants."

Harold Winters hung up, muttering, "Since when does a crowded hole-in-the-wall club like Scarlet's have potted plants? And I'm not old!" He was only forty-two. Mansfield-Smythe was in his late twenties. He supposed that did seem young to Beryl. "Comparatively speaking."

"Winters?" Felicia Montgomery, Winters' surprisingly petite top agent, poked her head in, a strained smile on her face. "There's some girl here. She says she's a new agent."

"What?" Winters practically fell off of his chair. "New— I haven't asked—"

A leggy brunette sidled in behind Felicia, her siren-red tank top and hip-hugging jeans painted onto her curvy body. "You didn't have to ask, Boss Man. I'm just a gift." She smiled seductively at the open-mouthed Guardian. "It's your lucky day, Mal," she purred, sitting on the edge of his cluttered desk.

Harold practically fainted with relief. "Malcolm! There's a... lady here to see you."

May 2006

"You wanna come with us to Scarlet's?" Felicia tried to make their recent addition, a field agent from the New York area, feel welcome. The entire male population of Creek Valley had certainly done their part.

Hope Maguire gave the smaller, sun-kissed blonde a sex-siren smile, her cherry-black lips parting sensually as she tossed her mane of dark hair. "Nah. Got a hot date."

"I'm surprised Mansfield-Smythe lets you off the lead," Nox was slouched in the back, polishing a lethal-looking blade. He never even looked up, or he would have caught the sudden bitterness on Hope's face. It wasn't a dig at the brunette Hunter, but her stick-in-the-bum Guardian.

Both his barb and his refusal to acknowledge her sex-on-legs posturing rankled more than she'd care to admit. No one owned her. And no way in hell she'd want a pasty, pale vampire, even if he was utterly fuckable, those sharp cheekbones, that accent, those eyes.... Nah. Screw it. Her Warrior senses went haywire whenever she was around him.

"Shut up, Nox. Winters paid you. To use the British slang you love to ruin my ears with, 'shove off.'" Felicia sent a withering glare at the Darkling turned informant-turned-occasional-backup.

No one needed to notice that the glare lingered, meeting his piercing blue eyes for a little too long.

Hope felt a whip crack in the middle of her spine. It was true. What the Rogues said was true.

Nox lifted his head, nostrils flared. Fear? Sex? Adrenaline? He kept his eyes on Felicia. "I'm not invited to Scarlet's, Huntress?"

"You're only here so I don't kill you and because we can't handle Guild business and Winters Interventions business at the same time. Someone must be brewing something." Felicia tore her eyes from his with an effort.

"Yes, so much so that you have to bring in the hired muscle and the slut bomb," Nox chuckled darkly. "And Guardian-the-Younger."

Hope, AKA the slut bomb, drew a stake from her waistband as casually as most would check their phones. "Well, since the slut and the Guardian are here, it seems like they don't need you anymore. I'll just save Winters some money." *And put a stop to what's brewing... Little Miss Innocent can't see the Big Bad Wolf wants to take a bite out of her.*

"Don't!" Felicia pulled Hope's elbow sharply.

"What's wrong, Valley Girl? I'll get you another vamp. One who knows his place." Hope shrugged the smaller woman's arm off, never losing her smile.

"I don't want another vampire! I don't want this one." Felicia felt truth wriggling in the back of her brain. She and Nox weren't friends or anything, but they had a mutual truce. They helped each other. Sometimes... sometimes she thought it might be worth giving her heart to someone again, or at least letting it out of its cage.

"You already had one vamp. That's what everyone says."

"Liam's a decent vampire. He has his human soul. He works for the Guild."

"Ooh, freaky girl." Hope cocked her head appraisingly. "I've heard some Warriors get off on it. The risk. The rush. Maybe I *should* try it myself." Her eyes lingered over Nox's taut body, rising slowly, blade resting on the bench at his back.

"Leave her alone," Nox said in a flat voice, resisting the urge to let his fangs slide free.

Hope's eyes traveled between Felicia and the vampire. Nox didn't have a soul, but he didn't kill. He had some "truce" with Winters and his privileged little pets. All of them were so cuddly close to one another, all "Besties" and "Bros." All bonded. Practically inbred.

Throw in the vampire.

Corruption. Contamination.

"Awww, look at that," Hope breathed. "Got yourself a pet, Montgomery? Is he a good little lapdog? Or more of a pussy?"

A lot of things happened at once. Nox lunged and growled, Hope's stake was raised again, and Felicia jumped in the middle.

"Stop! Nox helps us, he doesn't hurt anyone!" Felicia's fingers locked on Hope's elbows, forcing her raised arms to her sides.

"Mind your mouth," Nox snarled at the struggling brunette.

"I'm surprised she doesn't mind yours. You like the bites, Blondie?" Hope knew she was burning bridges. She didn't care. The Rogues would be in charge soon enough.

There was a crack and a snap. Felicia broke the stake in her bare hand, her Warrior strength on full display. "What the hell is wrong with you?"

"I was just going to ask you the same question. I'm outta here. I'll pass on the drinks. I'm not really into the red stuff," she panted, humiliated. That short little blonde couldn't necessarily beat her, but she could force her to a draw. Hope stormed out.

She was done with those losers.

"YOU WERE RIGHT. YOU guys were so right. They've crossed the line, all of them." Hope paced the gray box-like room.

"The first vampire was a warning. That the Guild ever accepted Montgomery's lover, even with his human soul restored... They wouldn't have if she and Winters weren't so influential. You see how that ended."

"Hot vampires. It's like the gateway drug, man." Hope chuckled grimly.

The shadowy figure continued. "Then the succubi. The witches. There's another vampire among them now, not a soul in sight. He killed several Heaven Fallen in the past, you know."

Hope didn't know, but she nodded as if she did. She never let anyone see a weakness, even a tiny one like ignorance of a simple fact. She'd had a Guardian once. Nice lady. Prim and annoying, rattling on about Mists and magics. She ignored most of it, except for the parts about monsters. She vaguely remembered hearing about Heaven Fallens, too, Warriors and Hunters that had died in battle and been returned to earth with extra powers, way beyond what normal Hunters and Warriors had. So Nox had killed some of them? More to the vamp than she'd thought.

"Nox is more than just an informant from what I've heard. He's bedding Winters' team leader?"

"Miss Perfect? Yeah," Hope lied again, comfortable with lies, far more than the truth. In the weeks that she'd come to be around the little group of agents, she'd come to hate them all. They all... pretended they weren't hurting. They were okay and happy, one big Partridge Family with a side of the undead. Felicia was the worst, a Warrior like her. Blondie clearly wanted to bond... but there was nothing they could bond over. Felicia was living a lie. Warriors and agents don't have friends. They don't have families. They don't have careers and dreams. Felicia still went home to Sunday dinner with her mother, for fuck's sake! She went to college. College.

Like a real girl. Normal girl.

"Maguire, if you don't want this chance, I have a dozen agents more experienced and willing. Let's not forget that you failed to keep your last Guardian alive." The man in the shadows spoke, leaning forward to reveal gray stubble and pulled tight over long jaws.

Hope swallowed hard. That was a low blow, but she deserved it. Her Guardian had been the first one to believe she wasn't some psycho chick, some drug-whore, seeing monsters. She helped Hope to get out of the last mental health facility the state had put her in. They worked together for a little over three months before a demon ripped the middle-aged Guardian in half, right before Hope's horrified eyes.

She was only nineteen when it happened.

She was twenty now, a lifetime in months, barely a year, turning harder than she already was.

I'm an effing diamond.

"I want this chance. Tell me what to do. I'll put that vamp in the ground, you know I can. I've killed—"

"I know you've killed many demons in your short time as a Warrior." The man rose. "I'm sure the Guild has been appropriately grateful?"

Hope hesitated. She ran after her Guardian's body hit the ground, unable to look at the two halves, still twitching. Abandoning her post and turning to her more familiar lifestyle of running, taking, and stealing for survival, the Guild had paid her nothing for the better part of a year. She would have a few weeks' pay soon, now that she'd reluctantly reported to the cardboard cutout, Mansfield-Smythe.

"They're grateful enough," Hope shrugged.

"But we are more so. We are exceedingly grateful to have you as our ally. We can pay you handsomely, take care of you as you deserve to be cared for, an asset, not merely an accessory."

Honeyed words, spoken in a factual voice, a tiny current of the trans-Atlantic running through it. Winters and Mansfield-Smythe had enough toys in their sandbox. She was a lone wolf, meant to stand out. Meant to be feared.

"I'll do it. Anything you say."

"Welcome to the Rogues." The man extended his hand, the rest of his body still bathed in shadow, a key in his palm. "I believe you'll enjoy your new accommodations, a luxury flat. Far better than the slum you've been bunking in."

Hope's cheeks flushed. They knew where she was staying? "Sounds good. What do I call you?"

"Sir."

He rattled her. She never showed that. "Oooh. I could dig it. Strong, silent… shadowy. Strong hands. Strong other things?" Maybe a little spanking, a little choking, a lot of hair-pulling…. She was tired of men who couldn't keep up. She'd guess from his voice that he was in his late fifties, early sixties, way too old for her tastes, but her tastes hadn't always mattered when she needed to trade favors. Powerful, though. Obviously powerful. She liked taking the powerful men to their knees, even if they made her get on hers first. "Why don't you come over here, Baby, and show me?" Sex was a good way to keep them off-balance, too. They thought they were the predators, but oh no. These days, men were always her prey.

"Stop. That sort of talk is detrimental to the cause. There will be no fraternization." The man's voice rang with contempt.

"Sorry. Sir." She hated that word. Both words, actually. Sorry was a word for losers. Well, losers who would admit they were losers. "What's my assignment, Sir? I've infiltrated. Informed."

"You've burnt your bridges there, Maguire. They'll never welcome you back into the fold now."

Hope felt a shiver run through her sinuous body, not the erotic kind she liked. As much as she hated them, Montgomery and her little crew had tried. Mansfield-Smythe was a prick, but he never hurt her. Aside from the demons, they were good people. Even the demons were pretty harmless.

She could never admit mistakes. Back to that weakness thing. Hope waited in silence for the man to answer her question.

"Winters is being controlled and corrupted. Whether he is aware or not, we can see what's happening, not with that foolish demon-worshipping witchcraft, but with pure science. The energy disturbances are worsening considerably. Soon there will be a Realm Rift, if not a full tear, a total breach. Winters and his team are no longer fit to safeguard this CrossRealms. The Guild itself is not fit. They've been hoodwinked into believing that association with Darklings can be tolerated. It cannot. If they're not stopped, we may lose Creek Valley to the Hell Realm."

Hope swallowed. "That would suck."

He ignored her attempt at understatement. "It's time for new blood to control our efforts in the Mortal Realm. The Guardians are stagnated and weak, misaligned." The English accent grew more pronounced. So did the glint of madness in the gray-blue eyes. "The Rogues must control the California CrossRealms, or we may lose this town, then the state. Demons will flood the realm and spread. We must not be stopped by half-efforts."

"Yes, Sir." This sounded like action. Hardcore, the war is on, guns-a-blazing action. The shiver returned, this time moving lower, resting between her hips.

"Winters' agents are too loyal to him to turn him over to the Guild or to stand down for the Rogues."

"Yeah, I've seen that. It's sick. He's Daddy Dearest to all of them. And that snotty twerp, Mansfield-Smythe, is bad news in a whole different way."

"Precisely. He'll be recalled soon."

"He will?" Hope frowned briefly. How did this guy know the Guild's plans for their prim and proper Poster Boy?

"It's customary to recall the Guardians of a post for debriefing after a tragedy. Once we're in charge, he'll have no need to return"

"What? What tragedy?" Hope shook her head. Had she lost the thread? They were going to prevent the tragedy before it could happen. She hated being called a hero or anything sappy like that, but that was kind of her deal— even if she was pretty bad at it.

"The death of Mr. Harold Winters. I expect him to be removed within the week. I'd appreciate it if you could take out the blonde bitch, too. The wiccas, as well. The succubus and the vampire are a matter of course. The rest are of little consequence."

"But... Winters is a human." Hope cocked her head, stomach churning.

"And?"

"And... I...."

"I don't have time for him to die a natural death. And of course, since you know my desires, I'm afraid I can't really wait for you to die a natural death, either."

Hope jumped at the unmistakable click of a safety going off. "I'll do it."

"Excellent." The man let her see a cold smile for a split second. "Then, when I appoint a new Guardian, I shall place you as his chief agent."

"Guardian?" She cocked her head.

He waved away the slip of a tongue impatiently. "For want of a better term. A Rogue Commander. Now, go. Don't try to contact me. I will contact you. After all," he handed her a piece of paper with an address typed on it, "I know where you live."

Read the next page for an excerpt from: It's Business, Baby by S.C. Principale.

It's Business, Baby

Benni Browne never left her house without two essentials— being dressed to slay and having her Bluetooth nestled over her ear, concealed by her perfectly styled hair. Her grandmother, the woman who had raised her and inspired her to push herself every minute of every day, fretted that her thirty-something granddaughter would die before she was forty.

"Baby girl, that thing will give you a brain tumor or the calls themselves are gonna give you a heart attack," Nana G scolded on a weekly basis.

Benni smiled, stepping into her black Mercedes and switching the headset to come through her car's speaker. "Nana, you say that every Friday."

"What else do I say?" her warm, brown sugar voice prompted.

"When am I coming home, when am I going to find a man, and when am I going to have a baby?" Benni checked her sunset red lipstick in the mirror. Perfection. Of course. The president and owner of Body By Browne made sure she was never seen without representing the best of her fashion line. Her taupe heel (bearing the telltale interlinking Bs on the instep) pressed the gas as she reversed out of her parking garage.

"Oh, I don't care so much about the baby, Baby."

They shared a laugh. Nana G was one of the few people Benni bothered to take time to laugh with these days.

"Work-life balance. Dr. Pat on the Hope Network was saying—"

"Nana, Dr. Pat is a quack. You raised me to slay all day, and I do! I have something to tell you." The excitement in Benni's voice told anyone who knew her that she was about to talk business. Pretty much anytime Benni's mouth was open, the comments were either about fashion or business, which went hand-in-hand to her.

"Ooooh, you met someone!"

"No!" Benni swallowed a huff of impatience as she purred past a series of high-rises for the elite, the sky still streaked with stars. Benni didn't believe in pushing anyone harder than she was willing to push herself. That meant she was the first one in the office each morning and the last one out each night. "Nana, this is about the company!"

"Isn't it always?"

Benni ignored that. "I'm getting the cover of *Businesswoman* next month. They did the interview yesterday and the photoshoot next week. They're going to come to the factory and the board meeting... A full four-page spread. The *cover*! Last year, I made the city's Forty Under Forty list. Now, *Businesswoman*. Next? *Forbes* or *Fortune,* Nana!"

Her grandmother crowed with pride and gushed over her success. Benni held each word like a warm blanket, adding layers around her heart. She had to admit, she'd sacrificed a lot to get those accolades. She'd shut out a lot of time-wasters and dropped a lot of friendships that simply wouldn't add to her prestige.

"Okay, Nana, I'm here. I need to get in and get the coffee on." Benni pulled into the parking spot that read: Reserved for Benni Browne, President. She checked her hair and transferred audio back to her headset once again. "I'll come over for dinner next weekend, I promise. I just need to get the spread first. I have a new textile supplier starting, too. It's too crazy this week."

"You always say that. It's too crazy. You're driving that train, Benni! Make it less crazy."

"Hey, this company runs like a well-oiled machine!" Benni beeped the car's alarm and strode into the building, shoulders back in her curve-hugging yellow dress, mocha silk scarf around her waist perfectly accenting her skin color.

In the glassy door's reflection, she grinned, a look somewhere between Cheshire Cat and hunting shark, wide hips and full bust swaying with each step, her body a clock's pendulum. *This is* my *time.*

"Then when you say it's crazy, that means *you're* the crazy," Nana said sternly. "No one is prouder of you than me, but no one is more worried about you than me, either. Your millions aren't going to keep you warm, your magazine covers aren't going to dry your tears when life gets hard."

"Well, they could. But the ink would run and no one wants that," Benni smothered a laugh. Her grandmother was being serious. A single parent, then a single grandparent, she was probably projecting her own sadness.

"Are you sassing me, young lady?"

"No, ma'am!" Benni swallowed audibly. She could bring a boardroom to their collective knees with one perfectly sculpted eyebrow, but Nana G could torpedo her with a single, dangerous rise in her normally sweet voice. "I know what you mean. I do. I'll keep it in mind and I'll see you next weekend?"

"Talk to you tomorrow morning, Baby Girl. Love you."

"Love you, too."

BENNI MOVED THROUGH her office and set up her morning meetings, started the coffee, and checked the quarterly reports. This week, she had three priorities. One, ensure the talking points in her interview could be backed up by glossy photographs of her design room, the warehouse, her boardroom, and the design floor. Two, get the new textile supplier on the phone and push him off his lazy ass. (She assumed it was lazy, as she'd struggled for months with his predecessor and had been instrumental in getting him terminated after multiple delayed shipments.) Third, make sure the product was going out. That was usually priority number one, but for one week, it could take third place. As an afterthought, she had better make sure to call a department head meeting and explain that this week above all weeks, she didn't need to be bothered with the small shit.

II

"MAVERICK TEXTILES, Marco speaking."

"This is Body By Browne President and Owner Benni Browne speaking." Benni didn't believe in the slow intro. Tell them who you are, then what you want. That's the only way to get ahead, plow through, and don't pick up any deadweight. "We have a shipment of poly silk that's been pushed back three times. I need it by Friday, or I'm cutting your contract."

The man on the other end of the call was silent for a beat. Then, he laughed. Laughed!

No one laughed at Benni Browne unless she told a good joke— and she didn't joke.

"I'm going to need you to do some fast-talking with OPEC and the Shaoxing textile bosses. Call me when you have a shipment of petroleum ready to convert."

Convert? Petroleum? "I have a huge area of my fall line stalled because I need that material," she explained simply. "The world's oil usage is not my problem."

"Mine, either. I take public transport when I can."

BEnni stifled a groan. "Do you want this contract, Mr.—"

"Mercado. Marco Mercado, Head of Maverick Textiles."

Benni swallowed. She knew all of her suppliers, she made a point of it. Suddenly talking to the head honcho didn't unnerve her (nothing unnerved her) but it threw her for a moment. "I usually deal with Mr. Leonard in Supply."

"Mr. Leonard was fired, largely due to your complaints. I told Supply that I will personally handle any calls from Body By Browne."

"Then you can personally handle getting me that product or returning my money and canceling my account with you." She was bluffing. There was no way she would willingly walk away from a supplier this late in the spring, not with a huge chunk of her fall line hanging in the balance.

"You can walk. I'd feel bad for your customers if you did. Every other textile merchant on the eastern seaboard is in the same position. Supply chain snafus and soaring oil prices, not to mention the tense political climate in the Shaoxing textile industry— everyone is hurting for China-sourced materials or polyester products, Ms. Browne."

Benni wasn't unreasonable. She would feel bad for her clients, too. For one thing, Body By Browne was one of the few lines that made daring, sexy clothes for all sizes, particularly the curvy women who still needed to rock a hot mini-dress at the club or kill it in a boardroom-smashing suit. She could see that Marco had valid points. However, she rarely conceded any points that could lead to failure. "But you're working on the problem, aren't you?"

"Of course!"

"Then call me back. I want a status report. *Hourly*. I want that material here by Friday, or I'll cancel your contract, and I'll want my entire deposit back— failure to deliver consumables."

She heard a long, slow whoosh of air. Marco was breathing through his nose. His lips were probably pressed down to a narrow line, jowls wagging with fury. She didn't know what he looked like, but she imagined some fifty-year-old stuffed-shirt barely holding onto his blood pressure because he wasn't used to dealing with a savvy businesswoman who didn't take shit and came equipped with a hefty dose of Black Girl Magic.

"This is the best number to call you on?" Marco answered.

Again, she was off her stride, but she didn't show it. "This is my direct line, yes." It was her business line and her cell. They were one and the same. She had a landline phone at home, but no one but Nana G called her on it.

"Then I'll talk to you at ten. And eleven. And noon. You're going to get sick of my voice, Miss Browne."

"Then you'd better move faster, Mr. Mercado." She snapped a perfectly manicured nail up to her Bluetooth and pressed the button to end the call.

Actually... Mr. Marco Mercado had a nice voice.

As she sat down to start hunting up another textile source on her laptop, her fingers diverted from their mission and typed, Marco Mercado, President of Maverick Textiles. She hit enter and watched her image search explode with photos of a drop-dead gorgeous Latino man in a variety of impeccably cut suits. The tailoring was topped off by sparkling brown eyes and a head of thick, raven-black hair that worked in waves to soften the wide planes of his forehead and chin and accent the knife-like ridges of his cheekbones.

Holy. Fuck.

Mr. Marcado was too damn fine to ignore.

Too bad she didn't believe in socializing with anyone in her business circle. Or anyone at all, period.